EASY RECORDER TUNES

Written and designed by
Philip Hawthorn

Edited by Jenny Tyler

Illustrated by Kim Blundell

Original music by Philip Hawthorn

Consultant: Stephanie Roberts

Music engraving: Poco Ltd., Letchworth, Herts

Contents

About this book

This book has lots of tunes which you can play on your soprano recorder. It will also help you to read and understand music better, and improve your skill as a recorder player.

In this book there are folk songs from all over the world, jazz tunes and tunes from classical music. Other tunes have been specially written. There are also tunes for two players.

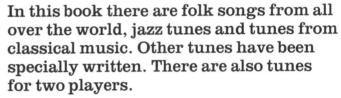

At the beginning, the tunes only use a few different notes. They use more as you go through the book. There are diagrams to help you get the right fingering for each note.

On many pages you can find out about music symbols and words. When you see an asterisk in the music, it tells you that there is something explained in a box at the bottom of the page.

The recorder comes from a very old family of instruments. You can find out about the different members of the family, as well as the ancestors of your modern soprano recorder.

There are a lot of interesting facts about many of the tunes in the book. You can also find out about some of the composers who wrote the music, such as Mozart and Beethoven.

Playing notes

Below are some fingering diagrams. These remind you which fingers to use to play the notes. They also show where the notes are written on the staff. Whenever there is a new note in a tune, there will be a fingering diagram for it.

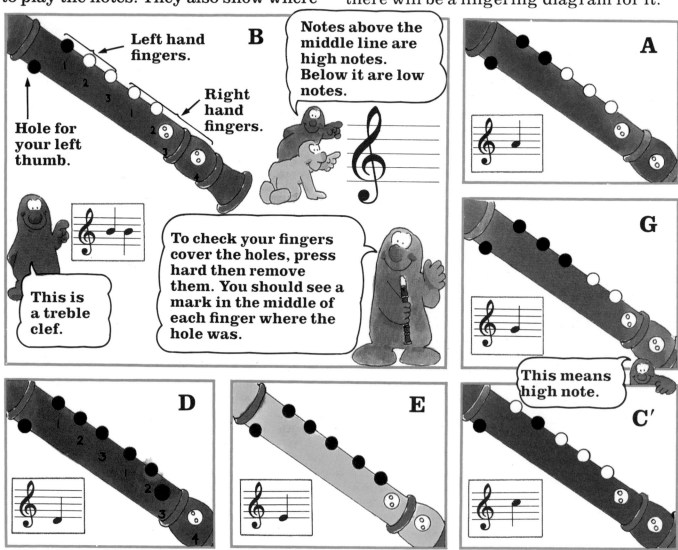

Your index finger is 1, middle finger is 2, and so on.

Sloppy Joe

Note lengths

Notes lengths are measured in beats. Below is a chart with three note lengths in it.

Quarter note

1 beat

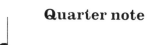
Half note

2 beats

Whole note

4 beats

Using your tongue to blow notes

Before you blow a note, put your tongue behind your top teeth. Now move your tongue as if you were saying "tah" as you blow into the recorder.

Hold the note for the correct number of beats.

To finish the note, put your tongue back behind your teeth as you stop blowing.

This is called tonguing. It gives notes a crisp start and finish.

Don't blow too hard or you may get a squeak.

Bars and time signatures

Music is divided up into bars. Each bar has the same number of beats in it. The numbers at the beginning of the music are called the time signature. This tells you how many beats in a bar, and how long those beats are.

This four means there are four beats in each bar...

this one says they are quarter note length.

5

The grand old Duke of York

The tunes on this page contain notes called eighth notes. Find out more at the bottom of the page.

This tune was popular in the late 19th century.

English

This was a clapping song. People used it to warm their hands.

Pease pudding hot

It was first sung around the year 1797.

English

Eighth notes

An eighth note is half a beat long. Clap the rhythm on the right as you say the words, then play it on one note.

Ice   is   ve —ry   nice

Don't rush them, they are the same length.

Eighth notes can also be written on their own.

7

Aiken drum

The tune below starts with an incomplete bar, called a part bar. Find out more below.

This tune is from an English folk song.

English

Sore feet

Play this tune quite slowly at first as it has a lot of eighth notes in it.

Part bars

When a tune starts with a part bar, count the beats that are "missing" in your head before you play. This will help you to get the rhythm right.

1, 2, 3, 4

In the top tune above, count three beats before you play the eighth notes.

A part bar is also called an anacrusis.

The last bar has the "missing" beats from the anacrusis.

Beachcombers

This tune has a high D (D′) in it. You can see how to play it below.

The distance between low D and high D is called an octave.*

The tune above has two beats to every bar. This is called double time.

Go and tell Aunt Nancy

This tune has four beats in each bar, called common time.

American

Octaves

Notes that are an octave apart sound similar. Listen carefully while you play D and D′.

D′

* An octave is the distance between any note and the next note above or below it that has the same name.

9

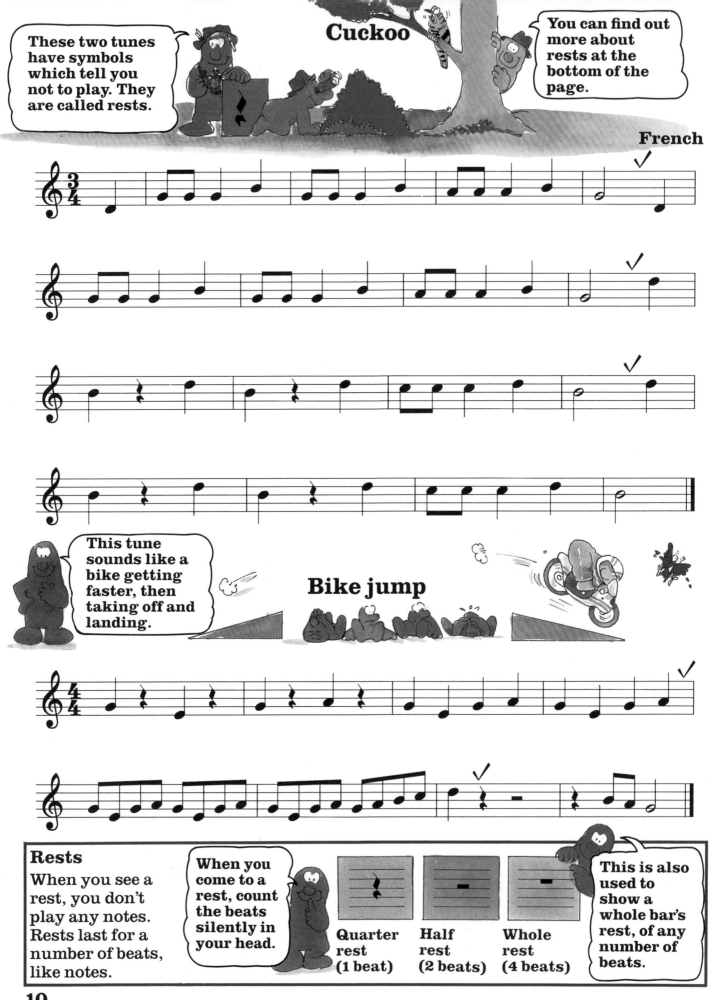

* Sometimes the note is called a "flat". Find out more on page 34.

Home on the range

There is a sharp sign next to the treble clef. It is called the key signature. Find out more below.

This cowboy tune was written in Kansas, America in 1860. It was a favorite of President Roosevelt.

American

Key signatures

When you see a sharp sign at the beginning of a tune, it is called a key signature.

It means that you play an F# whenever you see a note written on an F space or line.

This note is an F#.

A tune with an F# in the key signature is said to be in the key of G.

Tunes without any sharp signs in the key signature are in the key of C.

This key signature saves having a sharp sign written for every F#.

You can find out more about keys on page 32.

16

O come all ye faithful

English

Playing loudly and softly

The letters in music which tell you how loudly or softly to play stand for Italian words. This is because the way music is written today is based on the ideas of an Italian monk called Guido d'Arezzo who lived from 995 to 1050.

Soft words

These words are based on the Italian word *piano* which means soft.

Loud words

These words are based on the Italian word *forte* (for-tay), meaning loud.

19

Daisy Bell

Harry Dacre

Michael row the boat ashore

Traditional

20

Funky tortoise (Part A)

This tune has an Italian word at the beginning which tells you how fast to play. Find out more below.

This tune is part of some music for two players. Look at the next page.

This tune has these "first and second time" symbols in it. It also has a new note. Find out about them below.

Can-can

Offenbach was a French-German composer who lived from 1819 to 1880.

Offenbach

Italian speed words

There are many Italian words which tell you how fast to play. Here are some of them.

Presto means very fast.

Allegro means fast.

Andante means fairly fast, or "walking pace".

Lento means slowly.

First and second time

The first time, you play the bars with this written over them.

The second time you skip them and play the bar with this over it.

C#'

22

Funky tortoise (Part B)

This tune can be played at the same time as the one with the same name on the left. Find out more below.

It has a new note, the octave above low E. Find out more below.

D.C. stands for *da capo*, which tells you to go back to the beginning. *Al Fine* means "to the finish". Find out more below.

Au clair de la lune

The title means "by the light of the moon".

D.C. al Fine

Tunes for two players

Tunes for two people are called duets. You could play "Funky Tortoise" with a friend. One of you plays part A and the other part B.

Count a bar together before you start to play so you begin at the same time.

You could record yourself playing one part, then play it back while you play the other "live".

D.C. al Fine

You play the repeats as normal. When you get to the end of the tune, you go back to the start and play until you get to the word *Fine*.

This is the order in which you play the lines of music.

Line 1
Line 1
Line 2
Line 1

Playing high E

Play low E. Then slowly bend your left thumb so that the nail slides down.

Or uncover the hole by rolling your thumb down a bit. Both movements produce high E.

E'

Get whizzy, Lizzie

This tune has curved lines which join together notes on different lines and spaces.

These are called slurs. The notes they join are slurred notes. You can find out about them below.

Blues music began in America in the last century. Tunes are often based on 12 bar sections.

Moon buggy blues

Blues is based on a blend of African tribal rhythms and European folk music.

Slurred notes

With slurred notes, you only tongue the first one. The others are played by moving the fingers only.

Tongue this note..

..but not these two.

Tied   Slurred

Slurred notes are different from tied notes* because they are on different lines or spaces.

24   * If you want to remind yourself about tied notes, look at page 11.

Roller skater rag

Rag music is a kind of jazz. Jazz grew out of blues music at the end of the 19th century.

There are notes with dots over or under them in this tune. These are *staccato* notes. Find out more below.

In rags, play the second beat of the bar more strongly than the others. Rhythms like this are "syncopated".

Ali pally pogo

The tune above has these natural signs in it. They are explained below.

Staccato notes

Staccato notes are short ones. Instead of saying "tah" as you play, you say "tut".

Staccato quarters are like eighths followed by rests.

Don't get *staccato* notes and dotted notes mixed up.*

Naturals

This note is just plain C, or C natural.

Signs apply to all notes with the same letter name in that bar, but not the next one.

* Dotted notes are explained on page 6.

25

Ash grove

This folk tune has a symbol which tells you to get louder. Find out more below.

It also has a low C in it. This is the lowest note you can play on your recorder.

Welsh

With a swing

mf

mp

f *mf*

Getting louder

This is called a *crescendo* (cre-shen-doe). You get gradually louder from the start of the symbol to the end of it.

Getting softer

This is called a *diminuendo* (dim-in-you-en-doe). The symbol is the opposite of a *crescendo*.

Start getting louder here.

Stop getting louder here.

Start getting softer here.

Stop getting softer here.

Playing low C

Make sure you cover both small holes with your right little finger. Blow gently as it is easy to get a squeak.

Low C is written on a line below the staff, called a ledger line.

C

28

Heads, shoulders, knees and toes

This tune is from an English folk song called "There is a tavern in the town".

It has a low F natural in it. You can find out about it below.

Traditional

Butterfingers

The end of this tune sounds like something being dropped from a great height.

Remembering *cres* and *dim*

The picture below shows you an easy way of remembering which symbol is which.

The words *cres* and *dim* are sometimes used instead of symbols.

The wider the gap between the lines, the louder you play.

The narrower the gap, the softer you play.

Playing low F natural

F natural is quite tricky. Practice by playing it before and after other notes you can play.

29

Recorder disorder

Spooky boogie

The oldest recorder
The oldest recorder in the world was made some time before 1400. It was found under a 15th century stone house in Dortrecht, which is in the Netherlands.

It is about the same size as a modern soprano recorder.

It is made in one piece rather than two or three, like recorders today.

The recorder is now in the Gemeentemuseum in The Hague, Netherlands.

The wood it is made of is elm.

Patapan

There is a note in this tune called B flat. It has this sign. Find out more below.

French

Briskly

mf

This tune is sung on New Year's Eve in many countries.

Moderato means moderately fast. About the same as andante.

Auld lang syne

Scottish

Moderato

mf

f

Playing flats

Flats are named after notes they are next to, like sharps. A flat is called after the note it is below.

This note is B♭.

It is sometimes called A#.

Here is a good way to remember which is which: flats go down, like flat tires.

A

B♭ (A#)

B

B♭/A#

34

37

Scarborough fair

English

This is an old English folk song. Scarborough is a town in Yorkshire, England.

Morning has broken

English

This tune was originally a folk song.

It later became a hymn.

38

Wedding march

Wagner was a German composer who lived from 1813 to 1883. This tune is from his opera* called "Lohengrin".

It is often played at weddings, as the bride enters the church.

Wagner

Grandly

This tune has a G# in it. Find out about it on the opposite page.

Aria

An aria is the name given to a solo song in an opera.

Gently

* An opera is a kind of play in which all the words are sung.

Toreador

The first Noel

This is a traditional English tune.

Traditional

Christmas song*

W.J. Kirkpatrick lived from 1838 to 1921.

Kirkpatrick

Like a lullaby

*This tune is used for Away in a Manger in Britain.

43

From "Adagio"

Albinoni

Triplets

Three eighth notes with a "3" over them are triplets. You play them in the space of just one beat. Clap the rhythm below as you say the words.

I like — 1 beat
Tedd-ing-ton — 1 beat

Triplets are a little faster than eighths.

This note and two symbols are in the tunes opposite.

Trills

With a trill, you play the note and the one above it very quickly for the length of the note.

For example, when you see this..

..You play this very fast.

Accents

This sign is an accent. Tongue the note with extra force to make it stand out from the others.

A'

Ledger line.

Baroque recorders

Baroque recorders were similar to the shape of modern recorders. Many had very beautiful and extravagant decorations.

This one is made from ivory.

It was carved in 1704. The baroque period was known for its ornate music and building designs.

This tune was very popular in the late 19th century.

Grandfather's clock

Henry Clay Work

Andante

f

This is a traditional dance tune.

English country garden

English

Lightly

mf

mp

mf

47

51

53

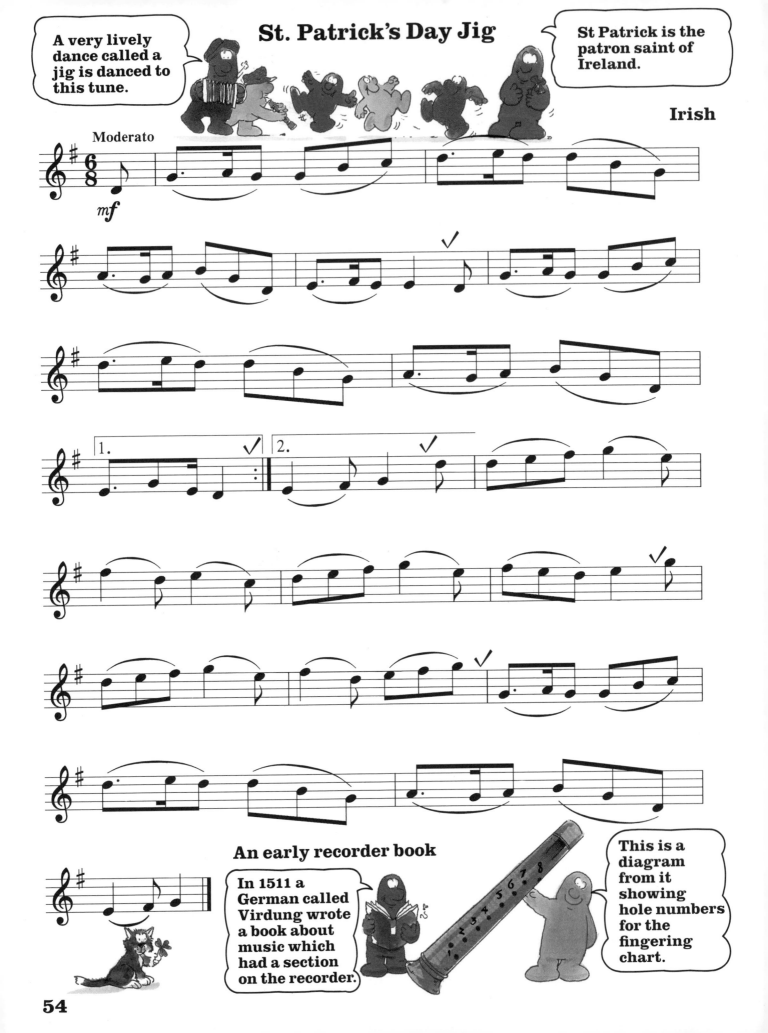

St. Patrick's Day Jig

A very lively dance called a jig is danced to this tune.

St Patrick is the patron saint of Ireland.

Irish

Moderato

mf

An early recorder book

In 1511 a German called Virdung wrote a book about music which had a section on the recorder.

This is a diagram from it showing hole numbers for the fingering chart.

Romance

Mozart

Minuet

Mozart

59

Shakers' tune

American

* You could also play the tune without the accompaniment.

Lullaby

The two small sixteenths at the end are called grace notes*. Play them very quickly.

Brahms was a German composer. He lived from 1833 to 1897.

Brahms

* A grace note is like an acciaccatura - play it before the main beat.

Music help

On this page you can see the music words and symbols that are used in this book. The index on the next page will tell you the page on which they are explained.

Speeds

presto	very fast	*andante*	fairly fast	*moderato*	moderately
allegro	fast	*adagio*	fairly slow	*cantabile*	in a flowing style
allegretto	not too fast	*lento*	slow	*ritardando*	slowing down

Symbols

repeat marks	‖: :‖	**grace notes**	♫	moderately loud	*mf*
dotted	♩.	**triplets**	♫	moderately soft	*mp*
breath mark	✓	**emphasis**		softly	*p*
tie	⌣	**accent**		very softly	*pp*
pause	⌒•	**tr**	*tr*	*crescendo*	<
staccato	♩•	**very loudly**	*ff*	*diminuendo*	>
slur	⌣	**loudly**	*f*		

Scales and key signatures

A scale is a series of eight notes from one note to the next one with the same letter name. Below is the scale of C major. The key signature is also called C major. It tells you which sharps and flats are in the scale.

Here are the names of other key signatures in the book.

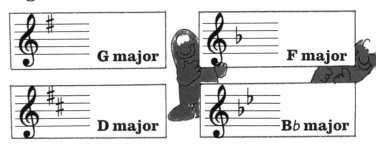

G major

F major

D major

Bb major

Fingering chart

Here is a chart which shows you the fingerings for all the notes in the book.

It also tells you on which page the note is explained.

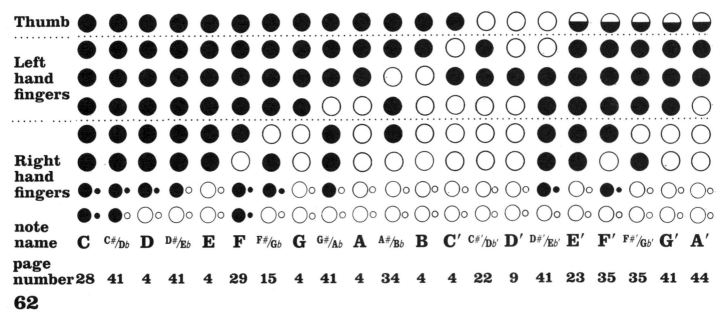

	C	C#/Db	D	D#/Eb	E	F	F#/Gb	G	G#/Ab	A	A#/Bb	B	C'	C#'/Db'	D'	D#'/Eb'	E'	F'	F#'/Gb'	G'	A'
page number	28	41	4	41	4	29	15	4	41	4	34	4	4	22	9	41	23	35	35	41	44

On this page there is some information about your recorder.

There are also some helpful hints for practicing music.

The soprano recorder

Below you can find out what all the different parts of the recorder are called.

The one in the picture has three joints, but some recorders have two.

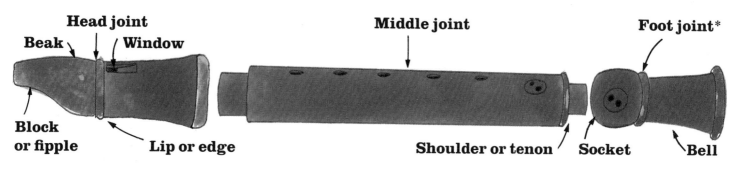

Head joint
Beak
Window
Middle joint
Foot joint*
Block or fipple
Lip or edge
Shoulder or tenon
Socket
Bell

Different recorders

On the right are the five most common recorders. The smallest, the sopranino, is about 9½in long. The bass recorder is about 35in long.

Sopranino
Soprano
Alto
Tenor
Bass
Crook
Key

The largest recorder is a sub-contra bass, which is about 10 feet long.

The smallest is the Garklein recorder, which is only 4½in long.

Practicing music

Before you play the tune...

Check the key signature so you know what sharps or flats to play.

Read through the music to check for music instructions and letters.

Tap out the rhythm of any difficult passages of the music.

When you play the tune..

Play through at a speed you can manage, even if you make a few mistakes.

Play the sections you found difficult until you get them right. Play slowly at first, then get faster.

Work at the tune until you can play confidently, without mistakes.

*On two-joint recorders, the middle and foot joints are one piece.

Index

First published in 1989 by Usborne Publishing Ltd, Usborne House 83-85 Saffron Hill, London EC1N 8RT Copyright © 1989 Usborne Publishing Ltd. The name Usborne and the device ☂ are Trade Marks of Usborne Publishing Ltd. All rights reserved. No part of this publication may be reproduced, stored in a retrieval system or transmitted in any form or by any means, electronic, mechanical, photocopying, recording or otherwise, without the prior permission of the publisher.
Printed in China   AE